SOROTCHINTZY FAIR

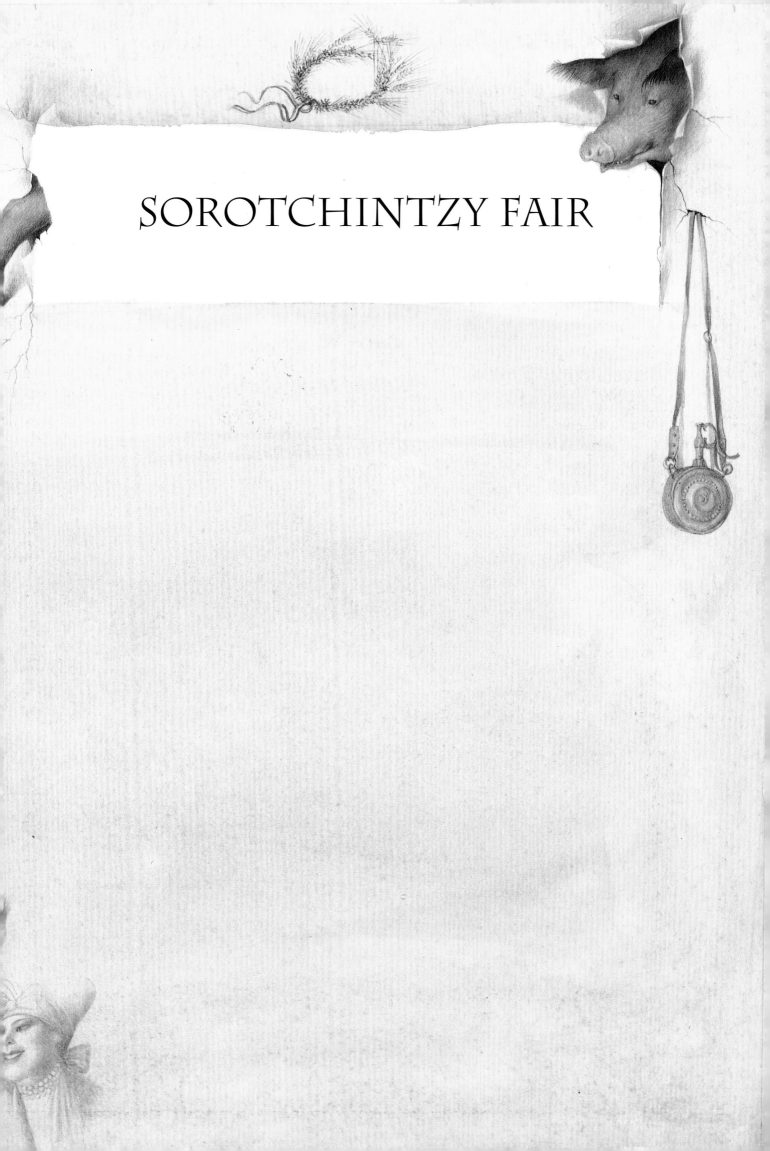

LCC Number: 90-84596
ISBN: 0-87923-879-8

First U.S. Edition
Printed in Belgium

Nikolai Gogol

SOROTCHINTZY FAIR

Illustrated by Gennadij Spirin
Adapted by Countess Sybil Schönfeldt
Translated from the German by Daniel Reynolds

David R. Godine, Publisher
BOSTON

…named Paraska was riding with her father, who was a farmer, and her stepmother, a vain and greedy woman, to the Fair at Sorotchintzy. Their wagon, pulled by an ox, was stacked high with things to sell at the Fair, and Paraska's father drove a mare that he also hoped would fetch a good price. The dusty country bridge was bustling with other wagons, as well as with crowds of people, young and old alike, on their way to the Fair. Clever lads sat on the bridge railings, seeing everything go by and making fun of it all.

The stepmother, buttoned up to her neck in a green wool jacket, and a magnificent bonnet upon her head, glared scornfully at the young people below. But Paraska, who was being allowed to travel to the Fair for the very first time, watched everything and everybody with great curiosity, especially one young man in a white coat, who had a friendly face and looked at her with dark and glittering eyes.

The wagon rumbled down from the bridge into the outskirts of Sorotchintzy. There they stopped briefly to meet up with an old friend the farmer hadn't seen for a long time. As they continued on their way, the noise of the city surrounded them with a roar like a waterfall. People shouted, laughed, and hooted in every street and alleyway. Cursing, lowing, bleating, bellowing — all the separate sounds joined into one huge uproar. Oxen, bulging sacks, piles of hay, gypsies, pots and pans, peasant women, gingerbread, caps — everything was bright and colorful. The excitement and confusion swam before Paraska's eyes. Buyers and sellers could be heard shouting in every corner of the market. Wagons creaked, iron tongs rang out, boards thundered as they were dropped to the ground. All this ruckus made Paraska's head spin, so that she hardly knew where to turn next.

Leaving Paraska's stepmother with the wagon, the farmer wandered around for some time among the crowds with his daughter. Her long tassels danced as she walked, and she had placed a garland of wildflowers on her head like a crown. Her father was thinking of the ten sacks of wheat and the old mare he intended to sell, but it was easy to see that lovely Paraska would have preferred to be over where red sashes, earrings, pewter crosses on necklaces, brass, and decorative coins were enticingly displayed.

She turned around and around, trying to take in all the sights of the Fair, when suddenly before her was the young man in the white coat, looking at her with his bright eyes. Her heart pounded like never before, but he reached gently for her hand and said softly, "Don't be afraid, dear heart, don't be afraid."

The farmer turned to speak to his daughter, but just then he heard the price of wheat being discussed behind him. He forgot about his child and mingled with the merchants, who, by now, were no longer talking about the price of wheat, but about the Devil, and a ramshackle barn where he was supposedly up to his usual tricks.

"Not a single Fair has come and gone in Sorotchintzy without some kind of trouble. Yesterday the town clerk came by late at night, and what do you think? A pig's snout was suddenly sticking out of the hayloft window! It grunted and snorted so loudly that it sent a chill up and down the clerk's back. Watch out! You can be sure that the Red Coat will soon appear!"

The farmer's hair stood on end, even though he had no idea what the Red Coat was. But just as he was going to pull his daughter close to him for protection, he saw that someone else had already embraced her: it was the handsome young man in the white coat. The farmer gathered his breath to scold him, but the young man quickly identified himself as the son of old Golopupenko, whom the farmer knew well, and asked for the beautiful Paraska's hand in marriage. The farmer was quite satisfied, and the three went happily along to the nearest tavern to celebrate the engagement with a round of drinks. Afterwards, the young man bought the finest wooden pipe, a flowered red scarf, and, as a gift for the farmer, a beautiful fur cap. Indeed, he bought presents for everyone who deserved them.

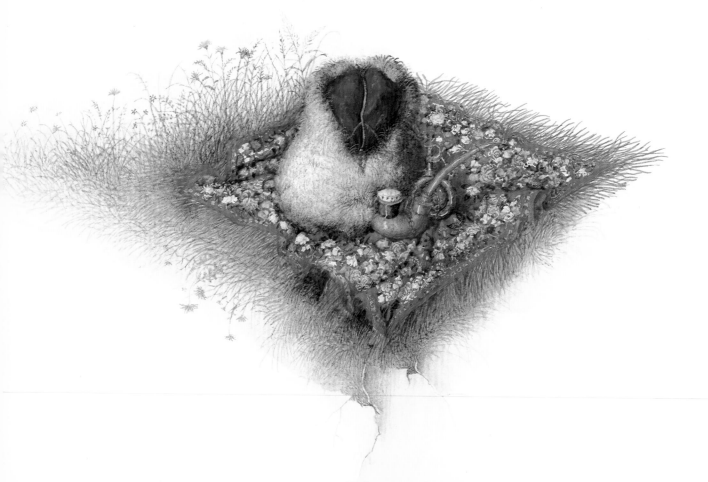

Back at the wagon, however, the stepmother was not pleased at all. "Well, well!" she shouted at her husband. "This is a wonderful time to be looking for bridegrooms! You fool, oh you fool! You should have sold your wheat instead. Won't he be a fine bridegroom — probably a beggar and a thief!"

She nagged and she nagged until the farmer gave her a solemn promise to undo everything. The beautiful Paraska cried; the young man stood sadly beside his ox and wondered what to do.

Then along came a gypsy, and whispered to him with a sly smile, "Will you sell your ox to me for twenty gold pieces if we get the farmer to give you Paraska after all?"

"Gladly!" said the young man, and with a handshake the deal was struck.

Meanwhile, a rumor had been going around at the Fair that the Red Coat had been seen somewhere among the wagons. A fright went through the crowds, and when night fell everyone ran home as quickly as possible.

The tavern, peaceful and safe, was filled with merchants from the Fair. Sitting near the warm oven, the farmer asked his old friend, "What can you tell me about this Red Coat?"

His friend answered with a sigh, "Oh, we should never talk about that after nightfall! But listen: One day the Devil was chased out of Hell, just like a dog chased out of a hut by a farmer. The Devil, though, got homesick for Hell — so homesick that he began to drown his sorrows in drink."

"What are you trying to tell me, old friend?" the farmer interrupted. "How could the Devil get into a tavern? After all, he has claws on his paws and horns on his head!"

"But that's just the thing about this story. He had a cap and gloves on, and a Red Coat, so no one recognized him. But he drank so much that he ran out of money, and had to give his coat to the innkeeper to settle his debt. 'Take good care of it!' he said as he left. 'I'll pick it up again in one year.' But the innkeeper didn't trust him, and wanted his money, so he sold the coat. But what do you know, one year later the Devil stood there in the tavern again and called out, 'So, let me have my coat back now!' But the innkeeper couldn't, so the Devil cursed him and conjured up a herd of swine to chase him, and they lashed the innkeeper with three-tailed whips and made him dance to their music until he whined and howled and finally confessed that he had sold the coat to a merchant woman. However, all the woman's luck had vanished as soon as she bought the coat, so she tried to burn it. Coats from Hell don't catch fire, though, so she hacked it up and scattered it to the winds at the very next Fair. That's why the Devil comes to the Fair every year in the shape of a pig, and grunts and looks around for the pieces of his coat. Now they say he's only missing the left sleeve...."

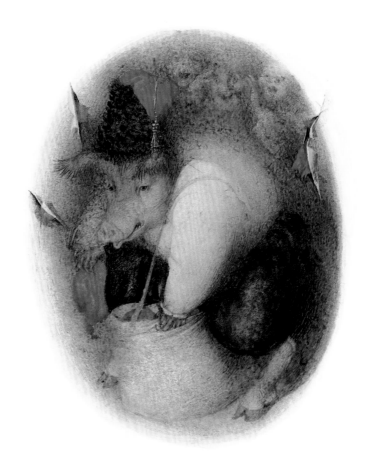

The farmer believed every word, and that night he pulled his down quilt all the way over his ears in sheer fright.

The next morning a fresh sweet breeze blew over the awakening town and his fear and horror vanished. The farmer went out to sell his mare. He stood in the street holding the animal and called out to passers-by. Before he knew it, a gypsy as tall as a tree stood before him and asked, "What are you selling, good man?"

The astonished farmer replied, "You can see for yourself what I'm selling!"

"Leather straps and straw?" asked the gypsy.

The farmer looked around him. In his hands he held only the reins, which had been cut through. And hanging from the reins — Oh, horror! the farmer's hair stood straight up — a sleeve from a red coat!

   As if chased by the Devil himself, the farmer ran through the alleys. But shouts of "Catch him!" had already risen up, and a pair of strong young lads grabbed him, tied him up, and accused the farmer himself of stealing the missing mare. They shoved him and his old friend, who had come to help, into a hut and bolted the door. The two of them lay there, tied up on the straw, but before they could start whining and complaining the young man in the white coat arrived. "What happened to you?" he asked. "Who tied you up like this?"

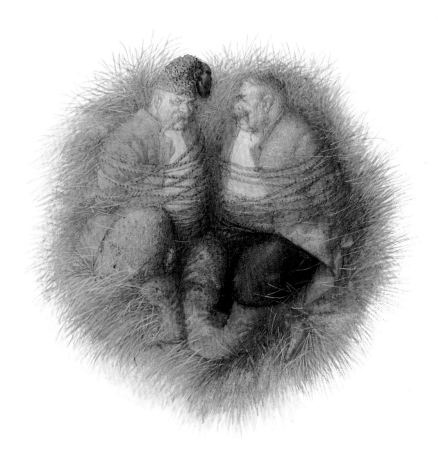

"Oh, you've come at just the right time!" the farmer cried out joyfully. "How could I have turned you away? Forgive me, good man! But what could I do? I can't do anything to oppose my wife."

"I don't hold any grudges," replied the young man. "If you wish, I'll free you, but in return, you must promise me one thing: the wedding! And we want such a celebration that feet will be aching for a year and a day from all the dancing!"

"Wonderful!" the farmer cried. "I'd be so overjoyed if we could all be together. No one can ever make me change my mind again!"

"Then I'll be at your house in an hour," the young man said. "And now, go home. Buyers for your wheat and your mare are waiting!" With that, he waved to his friends, and they came forward to untie the two men.

"Has the mare found her way back, then?" the puzzled farmer asked.

All the young lads laughed, and the one in the white coat said to the gypsy, "You've done your job well!"

The whole village celebrated the wedding. The ribbons in pretty Paraska's hair fluttered while she danced with her young and handsome husband. Late in the evening the songs became softer, and the sound of a fiddle slowly died off in the distance.